"All of these dogs want the same thing for Christmas," Conor told them. "A family of their own." Bonnie looked at a small brown Staffie with tiny ears and a little pink nose, then at one with big floppy ears, then at a dog that looked like a mixture of breeds – he had short fur and a long waggy tail. She wished she could take them all home!

"Belle's over here," Conor told them. Mum and Dad followed him, but Bonnie stayed smiling at the mongrel dog.

Suddenly she heard her mum gasp. "Oh, Bonnie!" Mum called. "Come and see!"

Bonnie waved a quick goodbye to the dog, then rushed over to Mum and peered into the pen. Belle was asleep in her basket, her belly up just like she wanted a tummy rub. As she heard Bonnie approach her ears twitched, and then she opened her eyes. She was a little white puppy – covered with gorgeous black spots!

"She's a Dalmatian!" Bonnie cried.

Have you read all these books in the
Battersea Dogs & Cats Home series?

SPARKLE
and BELLE'S
story

by

Sarah Hawkins

Illustrated by Artful Doodlers

Puzzle illustrations by Jason Chapman

RED FOX

BATTERSEA DOGS & CATS HOME: SPARKLE & BELLE'S STORY
A RED FOX BOOK 978 1 849 41760 0

First published in Great Britain by Red Fox,
an imprint of Random House Children's Publishers UK
A Random House Group Company

This edition published 2012

1 3 5 7 9 10 8 6 4 2

The Random House Group Limited supports the Forest Stewardship Council
(FSC®), the leading international forest certification organization. Our books
carrying the FSC label are printed on FSC®-certified paper. FSC is the only
forest certification scheme endorsed by the leading environmental
organizations, including Greenpeace. Our paper procurement policy can be
found at www.randomhouse.co.uk/environment.

MIX
Paper from
responsible sources
FSC® C016897

Set in 13/20 Stone Informal

Red Fox Books are published by Random House Children's Publishers, UK
61–63 Uxbridge Road, London W5 5SA

www.**randomhousechildrens**.co.uk
www.**totallyrandombooks**.co.uk
www.**randomhouse**.co.uk

Addresses for companies within The Random House Group Limited
can be found at: www.randomhouse.co.uk/offices.htm

THE RANDOM HOUSE GROUP Limited Reg. No. 954009

A CIP catalogue record for this book is available from the British Library.

Printed and bound in Great Britain by
CPI Group (UK) Ltd, Croydon, CR0 4YY

Turn to page 91 for lots
of information on
Battersea Dogs & Cats Home,
plus some cool activities!

🐾 🐾 🐾 🐾

Meet the stars of the Battersea Dogs & Cats Home series to date . . .

Bailey

Chester

Misty

Max

Daisy

Rusty

Snowy

Stella

Huey

Angel

Alfie

Cosmo

Coco

Buddy and Holly

Petal

Suzy

Jessie

Bertie

Oscar

Bruno

Sparkle and Belle

Sleepover Fun

"Jingle bells, jingle bells!" Bonnie sang at
the top of her lungs. *"Jingle all the way."*
Her friends Claire and Kirsty joined in,
bouncing up and down on Kirsty's bed as
they sang. *"Oh, what fun it is to ride on a
one-horse open sleigh!"*

"It's a bit early for that, isn't it, girls?"
Kirsty's mum said as she came in carrying

a plate full of pizza. "It's only October!"

"Exactly," Claire told her. "It's nearly Christmas!"

"It's OK, we can sing something else. How about something from *The Little Mermaid*?" Bonnie said, thinking about the film they'd just watched. "*Under the sea,*" she sang. "*Under the sea.*"

Kirsty's mum laughed and shook her head. "Have fun, girls," she chuckled as she left the bedroom.

Claire wriggled into her sleeping bag and zipped it up to her tummy. "Look," she giggled. "I'm a mermaid, just like Ariel!"

"Good – I'll have your slice then," Bonnie joked. "Mermaids don't like pizza."

"This one does!" Claire said, struggling out of her sleeping bag.

"What shall we watch next?" Kirsty asked, pointing at the pile of Disney DVDs on her bedside table. "*Toy Story* is the funniest."

"No, *Finding Nemo* is," Claire insisted. "Nemo is soooo cute!"

"You're all wrong!" Bonnie squealed. "The best one is *101 Dalmatians*."

"Just because it's got dogs in it," Kirsty teased.

"Not just any dogs – *Dalmatians*,"
Bonnie said. "They're my favourite dogs
of all. And there are one hundred and
one of them!"

"Are you going to ask for a dog for
Christmas?" Claire asked through a
mouthful of pizza.

"Ooh, yes!" Kirsty agreed, flopping
down on the sleeping
bag next to her.

Bonnie shook
her head sadly.
"My house isn't
big enough.
Mum says it
wouldn't be fair
to have a dog
when there's no
room for it to run
around."

Kirsty nodded knowledgably. "Mum has to walk our dog twice a day."

Bonnie gave a big sigh and made her voice sad and dramatic. "So you *have* to let me watch *101 Dalmatians* – it's the closest I'm going to get to a dog of my own!"

Kirsty and Claire both groaned. "That's it, get her!" Kirsty commanded, lifting up her pillow.

"No!" Bonnie shrieked.

"Pillow fight!" Claire yelled, lunging at her.

Bonnie giggled helplessly as her friends piled on top of her. Then she grabbed her pillow and joined in.

When Bonnie woke up the next morning in her rustly sleeping bag on Kirsty's floor, it took her a minute to work out where she was. Somehow she'd turned around in the night so that her feet were resting on Claire's legs. Claire was already awake, so Bonnie smiled at her as she sat up.

"Sorry!" she whispered.

"It's OK," Claire smiled back. Just then, Kirsty gave a huge snore and woke up with a start. Bonnie and Claire giggled as she looked around sleepily.

"Girls," Kirsty's mum called as she knocked on the door, "time to wake up. Your mums will be here soon to collect you."

Bonnie just had time to get dressed and have some breakfast before her mum arrived. She gave all her friends a big hug goodbye.

"Thank you for a lovely sleepover," she said as she squeezed Kirsty tight. "See you at school on Monday."

Mum plonked a woolly hat on Bonnie's head and wound a long knitted scarf around her neck. "I brought these for you," she said. "It's really chilly today."

When she got outside, Bonnie was pleased she had the scarf. The trees were bare and twiggy, and the wind rushed through the branches and almost blew her hat off. Bonnie didn't mind that it was getting colder and colder though, because that meant it was nearly Christmas! She shivered with excitement, and Mum put a warm arm around her.

"Almost home," Mum told her.

"It's lucky that we live so near to Kirsty and Claire," Bonnie said happily. "I can see them whenever I want, and it's really easy to go around to each others' houses." She gave a little skip as they arrived outside their house. "See, we're already home!"

Mum gave her a funny smile and busied herself opening the front door. "Good. In you go, love, and get warmed up."

"Hello, chipmunk!" Dad came out of the kitchen, drying his hands on a tea towel. He slung it over his shoulder and looked at Mum over Bonnie's head. "Shall we tell her now?"

"Tell me what?" Bonnie said excitedly, jumping up and down. "Tell me what?"

Mum sighed as she took off her coat. "I suppose so. Let's go and sit down."

Bonnie shrugged her own coat off and dumped her hat and scarf on top of it, then raced into the lounge after her parents. Mum and Dad were sat next to each other on the sofa, and Bonnie balanced on the arm. "Tell me *what*?" she asked again.

"Mum has got a new job!" Dad said.

"Oh, well done, Mummy!" Bonnie went to give her a hug, but Mum still didn't look very happy. "That's good, isn't it?"

Mum laughed. "Yes, very good. We'll
have some more money, and things will
be a bit more interesting for me. But
there is one problem; it's right over on the
other side of London, near to where
Daddy works."

Bonnie still couldn't understand why
Mum seemed worried. "Are you sad
because you'll have to
get up really
early?" she asked.

Mum shook
her head. Dad
leaned forward
and took Bonnie's
hand. "Mum and
I have been talking,
and since we will both be
working over there it doesn't make sense
to carry on living here. It would be better

if we lived somewhere more in the middle, close enough to your school but not as far from our work. So . . . we're going to move house."

Bonnie felt like someone had thrown cold water on her. A horrible shiver went from her head down to her toes and settled in her tummy. "But *this* is our house," she whispered. "I've lived here since I was a baby. And it's really close to Kirsty and Claire." She gave a little sniffle. "I won't be able to walk around and see them any more." Bonnie thought about moving away from her friends and burst into tears.

Mum pulled Bonnie onto her lap and kissed the top of her head.

"We're going to move across London, lovey, not move to the moon. You'll still be going to the same school, so you can see them every day there. It's going to be a big change, but Daddy and I think it's going to be a good thing. We'll even be able to have a bigger house."

"It won't be the same!" Bonnie sobbed. Then she jumped up and ran upstairs. When she saw her lovely room, with its pretty pink walls and everything just the way she liked it, she couldn't help crying all over again.

Number Twenty-Six

"With any luck, we'll be in a new house by Christmas!" Mum said happily as Dad drove the car across London. "Now, the next one we're going to see looks really nice," she continued as she looked at sheets of paper from the estate agent. "Look, Bonnie, it's got three bedrooms so we can have lots of people to stay. Kirsty and Claire can come over whenever you like."

Bonnie turned her head away and refused to look. "It's probably horrible," she said, crossing her arms. "The last house was."

"And that's why we're not going to buy that one," Dad told her. "You have to see some stinky places so that you know when you find a brilliant one. What's the thing they say in all your Disney movies? You have to kiss a few frogs before you find Prince Charming." He looked at Bonnie in the car mirror and made kissy noises.

"Dad!" Bonnie giggled.

"Just have a look around and think about it," Mum told Bonnie. "You never know, you might like it."

"I won't," Bonnie whispered under her breath.

"Here it is," Dad said as they pulled up in front of a tall house with a blue front door. "Number twenty-six."

"Ooh!" Mum exclaimed, rushing out of the car. "It's lovely!" Bonnie liked it too, although she didn't want to say that. It had a nice tree in the front garden, and the windows and door made the house look a little bit like a friendly face.

As they went inside, Mum got more and more excited. But Bonnie just felt worse as her parents looked around, measuring the rooms and talking about where things would go. The house was nice, but it wasn't *her* house. She just wished they didn't have to move at all.

As the estate agent started talking to Mum and Dad about knocking down walls, Bonnie slid open the patio door and went out into the garden.

It was much bigger than her garden at home, with wooden decking and a wilderness bit at the bottom with lots of trees. The grass was long and overgrown like a jungle, and it was covered in frost so it crunched as she trod on it.

It was so cold that her breath came out in clouds. Bonnie wandered over to the space where one of the fence panels had fallen down. She peeked through into the next garden, where there was a swing and a slide, and wondered who lived there.

"It's a big garden, isn't it?" Mum said, making her jump. "It's actually big enough for a dog to run around in, don't you think?"

"I suppose so." Bonnie nodded sulkily. But then she realized what Mum had said and looked up. Mum was grinning.

"We always said that you could have a puppy when we had more room for it," she continued. "And if we moved here we would."

"Really?" Bonnie asked. She didn't want to move, but it would be worth leaving her nice room and being further away from her friends if it meant that she could have a dog of her own. "Really? Are you serious?" she gasped again, suddenly feeling really excited.

Mum nodded and pointed to the top of the house. "That room up there, with the little window – I think that would be the perfect room for you. Do you want to see it?"

Bonnie looked up at the window and felt a rush of excitement. "Yes please!" she said, grinning.

New Beginnings

For the next five weeks, Bonnie's old
house was turned upside-down as they
packed everything into boxes. Mum and
Dad had bought the big house, and
luckily it was ready for them to move in
to straight away. Kirsty and Claire had
been really sad when Bonnie said she was
moving, but they had been very excited
about the dog. "Besides," Kirsty had said

practically, "we'll still get to see you at school during the week."

Bonnie cried as she said goodbye to her old pink bedroom for the last time. Even Mum looked a bit sniffly as they drove out of the driveway. "Bye, old house," Bonnie said sadly.

"Hello, new start," Mum replied with a smile. As they followed Dad in the removal van, Mum turned on the car radio and a Christmas song blared out. Mum tapped her fingers on the steering wheel in time to the music. Bonnie could just

about see the lights of the van in front of them through the rain. It was strange to think that everything in their house was packed up in there. It was only the afternoon but it was starting to get dark. Nearly every house they passed already had their Christmas lights up, and the streets twinkled and shone through the drizzle.

Everything is changing, Bonnie thought. *By the time it's Christmas, we'll be settled in our new house, and I'll have a puppy!*

"When can we get the puppy?" she asked Mum thoughtfully. "Are we going to a pet shop?"

"Well, Daddy and I thought that we should go to a rescue centre, not a pet shop," Mum told her.

"What's that?" Bonnie asked.

"Sometimes cats and dogs don't have a nice home of their own," Mum explained. "So a rescue centre looks after them until they find somewhere else to live. The one closest to our new house is called Battersea Dogs & Cats Home. We won't be able to take a puppy home straight away, which is good because the house isn't anywhere near ready yet – but we could go and choose the puppy soon . . . maybe tomorrow. I have already phoned them up to register."

"Tomorrow!" Bonnie said excitedly.

"*Maybe*," Mum said warningly. "*If* we get all the boxes in tonight."

"We will! I'll help!" Bonnie thought for a moment. "But will they have any Dalmatians?"

"Maybe not, lovey; we'll just have to wait and see when we get there. I know you like Dalmatians best, but isn't it better to get a dog that really needs us?" Mum asked.

Bonnie thought about how sad a puppy would be if it didn't have a family of its own, and nodded. She'd love *any* puppy, but she couldn't help hoping that she'd get the dog of her dreams. As the car stopped at some traffic lights she

looked out of the window at a
tall Christmas tree with a
shining star at the very top.
*I'll make a wish on a
Christmas star*, Bonnie
thought to herself, *that
there'll be a Dalmatian
puppy waiting for me
there.*

As they drove to Battersea Dogs & Cats
Home the next day, Bonnie fell into a
daydream. It had taken a while to
unload all the boxes and put them in the
right rooms, but Bonnie had rushed
around and helped Mum and Dad as
much as she could, determined that
they'd go and choose her puppy the next
day. Eventually it had all been done. Dad
had brought a bottle of champagne

home, and fizzy lemonade for Bonnie, and they'd toasted each other and the new house out of special tall glasses.

It had been strange going to sleep in her new room. Everything looked different, and the stacked-up boxes had cast a funny shadow on the walls. The bare branches of a tree outside her window had looked like fingers reaching out to grab her, and the wind had howled and moaned.

"Are you OK?" Mum had asked as she came to tuck Bonnie in. "I can find you a night-light if you want."

But Bonnie had snuggled down under her covers sleepily. "Don't worry, Mum, I'm fine. I'm going to dream about my puppy . . ."

"We're here!" Dad interrupted her thoughts.

Bonnie looked up at the blue sign with a cat and a dog curled up together. They'd arrived at Battersea Dogs & Cats Home! She leaped out of the car  and skipped all the way into the reception. The ladies behind the counter grinned as she burst in excitedly.

"We've come to find my puppy!" she told them.

"We've got an appointment," Mum said as she rushed in after Bonnie.

Once Mum had spoken to the receptionists, a nice man called Conor led them into a little room and asked them some questions about their new house, how much Mum and Dad worked and how often they'd be able to go on walks. Mum had told him that the new house was close to her work, so she could come home and walk the dog at lunch time.

Conor nodded. "We just have to check," he said, his blue

eyes serious. "Lots of people get a pet around Christmas time. They don't realize how much time and care a dog needs. We've just had a puppy brought in that the owner only had for three weeks before they decided that they didn't want her any more. Poor little Belle has been really upset since she got here. She doesn't understand why her old owner abandoned her."

Bonnie shook her head fiercely. "Poor Belle. I'd never do that. I know that you have to look after dogs and walk and feed them, but I still want one more than *anything*."

"Well, you seem like a very responsible dog owner," Conor laughed. "Right, that's all the questions. Shall we go and look at the puppies?"

Mum squeezed Bonnie's hand as Conor led them through the big blue door into the kennels. In each room there were several kennels with a dog in each one. As they passed, the dogs jumped up and barked, their tails wagging excitedly. Conor greeted a few of them as they went by, and promised to come back and take one out for a walk later. "We keep the

puppies through here where it's a bit
quieter," he said, leading them into
another room. Bonnie looked from one
kennel to the next in amazement.

"All of these dogs want the same thing
for Christmas," Conor told them. "A
family of their own." Bonnie looked at a
small brown Staffie with tiny ears and a
little pink nose, then at one with big
floppy ears, then at a dog that looked like
a mixture of breeds – he had short fur
and a long waggy tail. She wished she
could take them all home!

"Belle's over here," Conor told them. Mum and Dad followed him, but Bonnie stayed smiling at the mongrel dog.

Suddenly she heard her mum gasp. "Oh, Bonnie!" Mum called. "Come and see!"

Bonnie waved a quick goodbye to the dog, then rushed over to Mum and peered into the pen. Belle was asleep in her basket, her belly up just like she wanted a tummy rub. As she heard Bonnie approach her ears twitched, and then she opened her eyes. She was a little white puppy – covered with gorgeous black spots!

"She's a Dalmatian!" Bonnie cried.

A Spotty Surprise

Bonnie stared at Belle and her heart melted. "Dalmatians are my absolute favourite dogs," she told Conor, "but Mummy said you probably wouldn't have one."

Conor grinned. "You mum's right, we don't often have Dalmatian puppies here. There must be a bit of Christmas magic in the air. Let's take her outside to play."

Conor opened the kennel and Belle leaped up to come and meet him, jumping at his legs. *"Wruf, wruf!"* she barked in a tiny puppy voice.

"Aw, she's so cute!" Bonnie squealed. Conor clipped a lead onto Belle's collar and walked her out into the hallway. The little puppy paused when she saw Bonnie.

"It's OK, Belle," Bonnie said, kneeling down so she was closer to the little pup. Slowly, Belle came closer and put her paws on Bonnie's knee, standing on two legs to sniff all around her face and hair. Bonnie giggled as Belle let out a big breath that blew her fringe away from her face.

Bonnie looked into the puppy's deep brown eyes. "She is so adorable!" she gasped.

Conor laughed and they took Belle outside. "Come on, follow me," Bonnie told the excited puppy as she pulled the lead all over the place, peeking into the other dogs' kennels and sniffing at the doorways.

When they got outside, Belle rolled on the floor delightedly. It was sunny and not too cold, so Bonnie sat on the ground next to her and stroked her soft fur. Belle snuggled into her happily, all her earlier shyness gone.

"I can't believe that anyone would abandon you," Bonnie said softly as she stroked her.

Belle looked up, her deep brown eyes twinkling and her little pink tongue panting. Then she put her nose on Bonnie's leg. Suddenly her ears pricked up, and she started snuffling at Bonnie's coat. She jumped up, tail wagging, and raced around Bonnie, sniffing her all over, then started scrabbling at her coat pocket.

"Help, what's she doing?" Bonnie laughed.

"Have you got any food?" Conor asked.

Bonnie put her hand in her pocket and Belle barked excitedly. She felt around and brought out a wrapped sweet. "I didn't even know that was in there!"

"That's what she was sniffing," Conor told her.

"She must have a really good sense of smell." Dad smiled. "I hope she doesn't mind my stinky socks!"

"So, Bonnie, what do you think?" Mum asked, bending down to stroke Belle's back. "I don't think I really have to ask, but are you sure Belle's the one you want?"

"Oh yes!" Bonnie cried. "She's just perfect! Please can I have her?"

"Well . . ." Conor paused.

Bonnie gasped. *But my Christmas wish has come true*, she thought desperately. *Belle is meant to be mine.* Belle looked up at Conor with pleading eyes as well.

Conor laughed. "Don't look so worried, I'm only teasing. I was hoping that Belle would get a second chance with a nice family. Someone will have to come around and check that your house is suitable for a puppy, but as long as that's all OK, I think she's yours."

Bonnie jumped up and gave him a huge hug.

"Thankyouthankyouthankyou!" she cried.

"*Wruf! Wruf!*" Belle added, jumping around him.

Bonnie bent down and put her arms around the excited pup. "You're coming home with us, Belle," she whispered.

"Let's put her back in her kennel and we'll go and fill out the paperwork," Conor said.

Bonnie walked Belle back inside, happily telling her all about the new house. But when she got back to the kennel, Belle pulled on the lead and whined sadly.

"Can I talk to her for a minute?"
Bonnie asked. "I'll be quick."

The grown-ups all smiled. "OK," Mum
said. "We'll be over there."

Bonnie bent down so that she was the
same height as Belle and looked into her
eyes. "I know your old owner left you,"
she told the little pup. "But I'm coming
back, so don't be sad. I'll see you really
soon, I promise. And I'm never, ever
going to give you up. A dog isn't just for
Christmas, OK?" Belle's tail wagged
slightly. "You're going to be mine for
ever."

*

"I can't believe it!" Bonnie said as they walked out of the reception. "We've found my puppy – and she's a *Dalmatian*!" Bonnie twirled in delight. She just couldn't keep still!

As they reached the gates a girl with long dark hair came in with her parents and a little boy. "Please can we get a white cat, like Duchess in *The Aristocats*?" she asked her mum excitedly.

"Maybe," Bonnie heard her mum answer as they passed.

"Looks like you're not the only one who likes Disney films," Dad joked. "Although I'm pleased we're only getting one Dalmatian, not one hundred and one."

"If they were all like Belle I'd like lots of them," Bonnie said as she skipped along happily. "But I think there's only one as special as she is."

Settling In

"There!" Mum said as she hooked the last bit of curtain around the rail. "How does it look?"

Bonnie stepped back to inspect her new curtains. They were pink with big yellow flowers on them. "Beautiful," she declared. She loved her new bedroom. She liked the big built-in wardrobe, and the new desk that Mum and Dad had bought her. But most of all she liked her window. There was a big windowsill that was broad enough for her to sit on, and she could see down into her garden and even the garden next door, where the swing and slide were. It was too cold and wintery for anyone to play outside at the moment, but Bonnie hoped that she'd get to know her neighbours by the time it was summer. Maybe she and Belle could make friends with them!

It had taken lots of work, but finally most of the boxes were unpacked, and the new house was starting to feel like home. And just in time, because they were about to go and get Belle!

Ever since Conor from Battersea Dogs & Cats Home had come round and said that the house was a good home for a puppy, Bonnie had hardly been able to contain her excitement. And Conor had brought some other good news as well.

"It's the funniest thing," he had said when Bonnie had invited him in and politely offered him a cup of tea. "I've just come from your next-door neighbours' house. They're adopting a kitten!"

"What a coincidence!" Mum had exclaimed.

"We haven't met them yet – we've only just moved in."

"Well, this seems like a lovely house," Conor had said. "Will you give me a tour, Bonnie?"

After Bonnie had taken him around, proudly showing Conor where her dad had fixed the broken fence panel, Conor had agreed that Belle would love living there, especially playing in the garden. They could collect Belle whenever they were ready.

Bonnie had begged her dad to let her go with him and pick Belle up. "She'll be scared if she doesn't know she's coming

home with me," she'd pleaded. Finally
Dad had agreed. And now it was time to
go and get her!

"Bonnie," Dad yelled. "Are you
ready?"

Bonnie ran down the stairs three at a
time. "Yes," she said, putting her coat on.
"I've got her lead, and some treats,
and I'm going to hold her really
still in the back of the car so
she doesn't jump around."

Dad chuckled.

"Right then – let's
go and get your
puppy!"

When they got back to Battersea, Dad spoke to the people in the reception while Bonnie hopped from one foot to the other impatiently, holding the new glittery purple lead she'd picked out for Belle. Conor disappeared into the kennels, and seemed to take forever coming back. There were Christmas decorations hanging from the ceiling that swayed each time someone came through the blue door. Every time they moved Bonnie's heart leaped, but it was never Conor with her puppy. Finally she heard Conor's voice.

"Here we are," he said as he opened the door. Then there was a familiar *"Wruf"*, and Belle launched herself at Bonnie, her tail wagging furiously. *"Wruf! Wruf!"* she barked, as if she was saying, "It's you!"

Bonnie laughed delightedly. She felt just the same – if she had a tail it would definitely be wagging.

"Come on, let's get you two home." Dad smiled.

Belle was as good as gold on the journey home. She curled up on Bonnie's lap, with her head resting on Bonnie's arm so that she could look up at her adoringly. She wasn't interested in any of the scenery or the Christmas lights flashing on the houses; she only seemed to want to look at Bonnie.

Bonnie couldn't stop smiling as she stroked Belle's silky ears and traced her

finger around her beautiful black spots.
"We're here," she whispered at last. And
with Belle there, for the first time the new
house actually felt like home.

As soon as they got inside, Belle
started bounding about, rushing from
one corner to another
and giving
everything a
really good
sniff.

"Come and
see my room,
Belle," Bonnie said,
but the little puppy
snuffled straight past her
and went into the kitchen.
Mum, Dad and Bonnie followed,
and laughed as Belle started scrabbling at
one of the kitchen cupboards.

"That's where I put her food!" Bonnie said in amazement as she opened the cupboard and pulled out the packet. Belle whined and pawed at it. "OK!" Bonnie grinned, opening it and giving her a snack.

"She really does have a fantastic sense of smell," Dad said. "You're a great sniffer dog, aren't you, Belle? We should hire you out to the police."

"Bonnie, why don't you take her outside in case she needs the loo," Mum suggested. "Then we can give her some dinner."

"OK," Bonnie agreed, heaving open
the patio doors and shivering as the cold
air hit her. But Belle didn't seem to mind.
She bounded out into the garden and
started exploring. Bonnie followed her as
she jumped off the decking and trotted
over to the fence.

"No, Belle," Bonnie warned as her dog
jumped up onto a wooden panel and
started sniffing it. Belle turned as Bonnie
called her name, then put her nose back
to the ground. "Come here," Bonnie
called, patting her legs. "Come on, let's
go inside, it's cold."

Belle looked at her, her eyes bright, and gave an excited *"Wruf!"* Then, still sniffing, she followed her nose over towards a bush by the side of the fence, her tail wagging slowly.

"What is it?" Bonnie asked. "Have you found something?"

"Wruf! Wruf!" Belle barked again. Bonnie went over and peered into the bushes. There, crouched down behind the leaves, was a gorgeous fluffy white kitten!

Meeting Sparkle

"Sparkle!" came a frightened shout from over the fence. Suddenly a familiar-looking girl about Bonnie's age, with long dark hair, ran into the garden next door. She stopped when she saw Bonnie and Belle and gasped, "Have you seen my kitten?"

"Yes, she's here, in the bush," Bonnie quickly told her. The girl started to

scramble over the fence.
Bonnie pushed aside
the branches to try
and get to the
kitten, but before
she could reach
her Belle rushed
over. Both girls
cried out as the
Dalmatian
puppy dived
past Bonnie
and into the bush
towards the little cat.

"Don't let her eat Sparkle!" the girl
next door cried.

"Belle!" Bonnie yelled.

The little cat shrank back as the puppy
approached, her green eyes wide. But
Belle slowly crept closer and gently

sniffed at her. Sparkle sniffed at Belle too, their noses almost touching so it looked like they were giving each other a kiss.

"*Wruf!*" Belle barked hello.

"*Meow*," the kitten replied.

Bonnie gave a sigh of relief. "Good girl, Belle," she told the puppy. Belle's tail wagged as she sniffed her new friend once more, and then curled up next to her.

"It looks like they've made friends!"

Bonnie laughed. "If I hold the branches back, you should be able to climb over and get her."

"Thanks," the girl said, wriggling her way into the bush. "Come out now, you naughty cat." She reappeared a moment later with leaves in her hair and the tiny white kitten in her arms. Belle followed behind, her tail wagging happily.

"I'm so glad she's OK," Bonnie's neighbour said. "She's not meant to go outside until she knows this is her home, but she must have slipped out the back

door when I was putting my bike away.
She's such an explorer. I've only had her
a few days and she's got into lots of
trouble already." She started climbing
over the fence back into her own garden.

"You got her from Battersea Dogs &
Cats Home, didn't you?" Bonnie said
shyly. "I think I saw you there."

"How funny that we were there at the
same time, and you've moved in right
next door! I'm Jayna," the girl said,
cuddling Sparkle. "Me, Mum, Dad
and my little brother Minesh
have lived here for ever."

"Bonnie!" Mum called
from the patio doors.
Belle went scampering
up to her.

"Here, Mum," Bonnie
yelled.

"Come inside, you'll catch your death of cold!" Mum told her.

"Coming!" Bonnie called back. "I'd better go," she said to Jayna.

"Do you want to come and play tomorrow?" Jayna asked. "You could bring Belle so that Sparkle has someone to play with!"

Bonnie looked at Belle, who was putting her paws on Jayna's legs so she could sniff Sparkle goodbye. "Yes please," Bonnie replied. "If Sparkle and Belle are friends, I'm sure we will be too!"

A White Christmas

There was a flurry of Christmas activity over the next few days. Bonnie was an angel in her school nativity play, with a gold tinsel halo resting on her blonde bob. On the last day of school, she'd given Kirsty and Claire their presents and promised to see them over the holidays, when they came over to meet Belle.

But best of all, Bonnie and Belle had

been spending lots of time next door with Jayna and Sparkle. The first time they'd gone to visit, Mum had been a bit worried about taking Belle and insisted that Bonnie keep her on a lead. But as soon as Jayna had opened the door, Sparkle had rushed up to say hello to her Dalmatian friend. The little kitten had rubbed up against Belle's legs, and Belle had bent down to gently sniff her, her tail wagging. "They *are* friends," Bonnie's mum had laughed.

"Told you," Bonnie said, smiling.

As their mums sat in the kitchen and chatted, Jayna and Bonnie had played with Sparkle and Belle. They threw balls for them to chase, and laughed as both their pets raced after them and tumbled into each other. After a while, Belle had started giving huge puppy yawns and

snuggled down on the rug in front of
Jayna's Christmas tree. Sparkle had
trotted over to her and nudged her with
her nose, then curled up in between
Belle's front paws. Bonnie and
Jayna had agreed that it
was the cutest thing
they'd ever seen in
their lives!

*

By the time it was Christmas Eve, Bonnie
only had two more presents to wrap –
Jayna and Sparkle's. She and Mum had
picked out an *Aristocats* pencil case for
Jayna, and a bright pink cat collar for
Sparkle. "Come on, Belle," she called to
her puppy. "You can help me wrap
them."

Bonnie laid
out the
presents
carefully on
her favourite
wrapping paper –
the one with reindeer on. But as she
reached for the sticky tape, a flutter at
the window caught her eye.

"Oh LOOK, Belle!" she squealed. "It's
snowing!" The snow was coming down so

thick and fast that the garden was
already covered in a layer of white.
Everything looked magical.

"I think we're going to have a white
Christmas!" Mum said, coming in
to look out of the big patio
doors. Bonnie couldn't
stop staring outside.
It was so
beautiful.

A scrunchy
noise made
her jump,
and Bonnie
turned around to
see Belle trying to eat the
wrapping paper. "No, Belle!" she giggled.
"But you're right: I do need to finish my
wrapping. Then we can take the presents
around next door."

As Bonnie sat down again, the
doorbell rang. "Ooh, carol singers!" Mum
said excitedly as she went to answer it.
But when she opened the door, instead of
happy music, Bonnie could hear the
sound of someone crying.

"Come in," Mum said comfortingly.
"What's wrong?"

Bonnie went over to the
doorway as Jayna stepped
inside, and gasped as she
saw her friend's tear-
stained face.

"It's Sparkle," Jayna
said between sniffles.
"She's gone outside
again. I only opened
the door for a minute, to
look at the snow, and
before I could do anything

she . . . was . . . gone." Jayna dissolved into tears. "Mum and Dad and Minesh went out to deliver Christmas presents but I wanted to stay with Sparkle. Mum told me not to go anywhere, but I didn't know what to do – Sparkle's lost!"

Bonnie rushed forward to hug her friend. Mum bent down to put her arm around her too. "Don't worry, you've done the right thing," Mum reassured her. "And I'm sure she'll turn up. We'll shake her food box. If she thinks she's getting fed she'll come running inside."

Mum started putting
her coat on, and
Bonnie put her feet
into her wellies.
"We'll find her," she
whispered to Jayna.
Jayna squeezed her
hand, but her face
was still worried
and sad. "I
promise," Bonnie said.
"Even if we have to look
all night."

"*Wruf!*" Belle agreed. Jayna burst into
tears all over again at the sight of
Bonnie's puppy. She bent down to hug
her.

"Oh, Belle," she whispered into the
puppy's fur. "Sparkle's lost."

Belle gave a low whine, then jumped

towards the door like she understood every word.

"Did she go out of the back door or out of the front?" Mum asked Jayna as she reappeared with two torches.

"Out of the back," Jayna sniffed. "But I've been calling and calling, and she hasn't come."

"Right then." Mum clipped Belle's lead on and handed it to Bonnie. "Let's go and find this kitten!"

Bonnie pulled open the patio door and stepped outside. It was freezing and already getting dark. More and more snowflakes were falling down, landing in her hair and brushing against her face.

Bonnie looked around desperately. *How were they ever going to find a white kitten in the snow?*

Belle stepped outside, lifting up her paws confusedly as they sank into the snow. She bent down to sniff it and sprang back as her nose touched the cold. It would have been funny if Bonnie wasn't so scared for Sparkle.

"Sparkle!" Jayna yelled.

Mum flicked on the torch and filled the space in front of her with a circle of yellow light.

"Sparkle!" Bonnie called too.

Mum started shaking some of Belle's dry food. Belle looked at it and whined, but Bonnie stroked her ears. "We have to find Sparkle," she whispered.

"Look in the bushes and over in your garden as well," Mum told Jayna. "She's probably hiding somewhere if she's a bit frightened."

Bonnie's heart ached as she thought about the little kitten all lost and alone, out in the snow. She went towards the fence by Jayna's garden, but Belle pulled on her lead and gave a low whine.

"Come *on*, Belle." Bonnie tugged gently on the lead again. But Belle had her nose in the snow, sniffing something.

"Come on," Bonnie said impatiently. "We've got to find Sparkle." She thought about Jayna's sad face. "We've got to find her, or it'll be the worst Christmas ever."

"*Wruf!*" Belle said, staring up at Bonnie with her tail wagging.

"Sparkle?" Bonnie said again.

"*Wruf, WRUF!*" Belle replied, just as if she understood. Bonnie walked back as Belle put her nose to the ground again.

She held her breath as she followed Belle. The puppy sniffed forward, little by little. Then Bonnie spotted something in the snow which made her heart jump – a tiny kitten paw print!

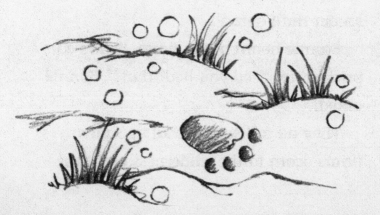

Merry Christmas!

"Mum! Jayna!" Bonnie yelled. "Belle has found Sparkle's paw prints."

"Sparkle! Sparkle!" Jayna called even louder than before.

Bonnie heard a tiny noise. Belle's ears pricked up. "Did you hear that?" Bonnie asked.

They all followed the kitten's paw prints down to the wilderness bit at the

end of the garden. Belle put her nose to
the cold snow again and started sniffing,
leading them over to the shrubs. *"Wruf!"*
she barked.

Mum held back the branches while
Bonnie crawled into the bush.

"Can you see anything?" Jayna said
anxiously.

Bonnie strained to look in the white
snow. "No," she said sadly.

"Come on out then," Mum told her.
Bonnie could hear Jayna crying again

and Mum comforting her. Bonnie sighed.
She'd been so sure Belle had smelled
Sparkle. She looked all around the bush
again, brushing away the snow and
pulling aside the snowy branches. As she
reached right to the back of the bush,
where it met the fence, a tiny movement
caught her eye.

Feeling a spark of hope, Bonnie
pushed herself even deeper into the bush
and lifted up a branch. There, curled in a
ball, was Sparkle,
looking cold
and afraid.
"*Meow!*"
she cried
miserably
as she
saw
Bonnie.

Bonnie wanted to shout for Mum and
Jayna, but she didn't want to scare
Sparkle even more. She carefully reached
forward and scooped up the tiny cat.

"She's here! I've got
her!" Bonnie cried
as she backed
out of the bush
with Sparkle
snuggled into
her arms.
"Belle was right!
We've found her!"
"Oh, Sparkle!"
Jayna burst into tears all over again
when she saw her kitten.

Mum hustled them all inside, and
once the patio doors were tightly closed,
Bonnie handed Sparkle to Jayna. The
little kitten was shivering and meowing,

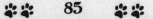

nuzzling her head
into Jayna as
she cried and
hugged her.

"Don't cry,
Jayna," Bonnie
told her, "Sparkle's
safe now."

"And I think she might have learned
her lesson," Mum told them,
disappearing into the kitchen and
coming back a minute later with some
food for Belle, some tuna as a treat for
Sparkle, and a mug of hot chocolate for
each of the girls.

"Now go and sit by the radiator, all of
you," Mum said, "and don't move until
you're nice and toasty again."

"I've never been so frightened in my
entire life," Jayna said as they sat down.

The radiator was lovely and warm
against Bonnie's back. Mum put the pet
food down in between them, and Sparkle
and Belle settled down
to eat, standing so
close that their
sides touched.
Belle gobbled
down her
treats and
Sparkle tucked
into her tuna.
When they'd

finished, Sparkle jumped up in Jayna's
lap, and Belle settled herself at Bonnie's
feet and put her head on her knee.
Bonnie sighed with happiness as she
sipped her hot chocolate. Everything
was OK now. Sparkle looked quite happy
as she curled up with Jayna, purring

contentedly. Belle reached over and gave her a sniff, and Sparkle sniffed her back, giving her another nose kiss.

"Aw!" the girls sighed.

"Thank you, Belle," Jayna said, ruffling the puppy's ears, "for finding Sparkle."

"And saving Christmas!" Bonnie added.

Belle looked up at them and give a sleepy "*Wruf*". Then she snuggled down next to Bonnie sleepily.

"Merry Christmas," Bonnie whispered, kissing Belle on her furry head.

"Merry Christmas," Jayna replied with a smile. "I already know what my favourite Christmas gift is." She nodded at the purring kitten, who was stretched out having her tummy rubbed.

"Oh, yes," Bonnie said as she looked at her sleeping puppy and stroked her velvety ears. "Now that I've got Belle, it feels like it's Christmas every day."

Read on for lots more . . .

🐾 🐾 🐾 🐾

Battersea Dogs &
Cats Home

Battersea Dogs & Cats Home is a charity
that aims never to turn away a dog or cat
in need of our help. We reunite lost dogs
and cats with their owners; when we
can't do this, we care for them until new
homes can be found for them; and we
educate the public about responsible pet
ownership. Every year the Home takes in
around 9,000 dogs and cats. In addition
to the site in southwest London, the
Home also has two other centres based at
Old Windsor, Berkshire, and Brands
Hatch, Kent.

The original site in Holloway

History

The Temporary Home for Lost and Starving Dogs was originally opened in a stable yard in Holloway in 1860 by Mary Tealby after she found a starving puppy in the street. There was no one to look after him, so she took him home and nursed him back to health. She was so worried about the other dogs wandering the streets that she opened the Temporary Home for Lost and Starving Dogs. The Home was established to help to look after them all and find them new owners.

Sadly Mary Tealby died in 1865, aged sixty-four, and little more is known about her, but her good work was continued. In 1871 the Home moved to its present site in Battersea, and was renamed the Dogs' Home Battersea.

Some important dates for the Home:

1883 – Battersea start taking in cats.

1914 – 100 sledge dogs are housed at the Hackbridge site, in preparation for Ernest Shackleton's second Antarctic expedition.

1956 – Queen Elizabeth II becomes patron of the Home.

2004 – Red the Lurcher's night-time antics become world famous when he is caught on camera regularly escaping from his kennel and liberating his canine chums for midnight feasts.

2007 – The BBC broadcast *Animal Rescue Live* from the Home for three weeks from mid-July to early August.

Amy Watson

Amy Watson has been working at Battersea Dogs & Cats Home for eight years and has been the Home's Education Officer for four years. Amy's role means that she regularly visits schools around Battersea's three sites to teach children how to behave and stay safe around dogs and cats, and all about responsible dog and cat ownership. She also regularly features on the Battersea website – www.battersea.org.uk – giving tips and advice on how to train your dog or cat under the "Fun and Learning" section.

On most school visits Amy can take a dog with her, so she is normally accompanied by her beautiful ex-Battersea dog, Hattie. Hattie has been living with Amy for three years and really enjoys meeting new children and helping Amy with her work.

The process for re-homing a dog or a cat

When a lost dog or cat arrives, Battersea's Lost Dogs & Cats Line works hard to try to find the animal's owners. If, after seven days, they have not been able to reunite them, the search for a new home can begin.

The Home works hard to find caring, permanent new homes for all the lost and unwanted dogs and cats.

Dogs and cats have their own characters and so staff at the Home will spend time getting to know every dog and cat. This helps decide the type of home the dog or cat needs.

There are three stages of the re-homing process at Battersea Dogs & Cats Home. Battersea's re-homing team wants to find you the perfect pet: sometimes this can take a while, so please be patient while we search for your new friend!

1 Register details

2 Match

3 Leaving with your new pet

Have a look at our website:
http://www.battersea.org.uk/dogs/ rehoming/index.html for more details!

Jokes

WARNING – you might get serious belly-ache after reading these!

What do you get when you cross a dog and a phone?
A golden receiver!

What is a vampire's favourite dog?
A Bloodhound!

What kind of pets lay around the house?
Car-pets!

What's worse than raining cats and dogs?
Hailing elephants!

What do you call a dog that is a librarian?
A hush-puppy!

What do you get when you cross a mean dog and a computer?
A mega-bite!

Why couldn't the Dalmatian hide from his pal?
Because he was already spotted!

What do you do with a blue Burmese?
Try and cheer it up!

Why did the cat join the Red Cross?
Because she wanted to be a first-aid kit!

What happened to the dog that ate nothing but garlic?
His bark was much worse than his bite!

What do you get if you cross a dog with a Concorde?
A jet-setter!

What do you call a cat that has swallowed a duck?
A duck-filled fatty puss!

Did you hear about the cat that drank five bowls of water?
He set a new lap record!

Did you hear about the cat that swallowed a ball of wool?
She had mittens!

Dos and Don'ts of looking after dogs and cats

Dogs dos and don'ts

DO

- Be gentle and quiet around dogs at all times – treat them how you would like to be treated.
- Have respect for dogs.

DON'T

- Sneak up on a dog – you could scare them.
- Tease a dog – it's not fair.
- Stare at a dog – dogs can find this scary.
- Disturb a dog who is sleeping or eating.

- Assume a dog wants to play with you. Just like you, sometimes they may want to be left alone.
- Approach a dog who is without an owner as you won't know if the dog is friendly or not.

Cats dos and don'ts

DO
- Be gentle and quiet around cats at all times.
- Have respect for cats.
- Let a cat approach you in their own time.

DON'T
- Stare at a cat as they can find this intimidating.

- Tease a cat – it's not fair.
- Disturb a sleeping or eating cat – they may not want attention or to play.
- Assume a cat will always want to play. Like you, sometimes they want to be left alone.

What to think about before getting a dog!

Here is a list of things that you need to think about before getting a dog. See if you can find them in the word search and while you look, think why they might be so important. Only look for words written in black. They can be written backwards, diagonally, forwards, up and down, so look carefully and GOOD LUCK!

```
I N D E P E N D E N T U N O P M S D H W
S X C V B N H R D G H I L J A N E V X Q
S F T I M E A L O N E N M K E R Q U S P
G T H S W V B J P X Z D F E H I Y J T M
A C V B O M G D F D S C T Y A A O P R W
F R O U Z C H I L D R E N C Y L I O A K
G D Y B I D F J L Q W E V Z L C O Z N R
M U I L D F G O H K V M F E T Y J K E M
A G H D N C V U B C V P O G M T R I R O
L W X D Z V G S I Z E B F C E X P Z S I
E T Q U A D B E H D L N K Y A G E J G L
O R J C O A T T Y P E N B C X S T F H J
R J U T G D X R F H K U F D G Z S G O D
F O R X A O K A Q E N S N M Y I E Q Z L
E N E R G E T I C P A S V H B N H X X K
M W D F B V H N L K G R U O I V A H E B
A S Q E T R Y I D A C X B U K O Y T F C
L Q D S T R O N G W I L L E D N J M X Z
E H G V N H K G N I N I A R T C I S A B
```

Can you think of any other things? Write them in the spaces below.

SIZE
MALE OR FEMALE
AGE
COAT TYPE
COST
BEHAVIOUR
BASIC TRAINING
HOUSE TRAINING
TIME ALONE
GOOD WITH: PETS, CHILDREN, STRANGERS, DOGS
HOW: ENERGETIC, CUDDLY, STRONG WILLED, INDEPENDENT

Remember: when training a dog, reward works better than punishment.

Tangled Leads and Crazy Maze

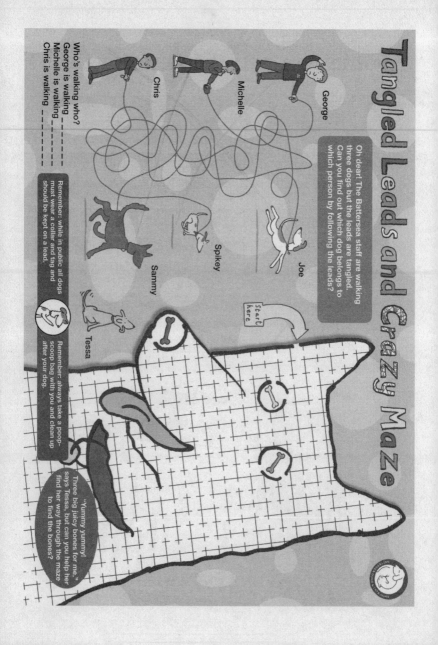

Oh dear! The Battersea staff are walking three dogs but the leads are tangled. Can you find out which dog belongs to which person by following the leads?

George

Michelle

Chris

Spikey

Joe

Sammy

Tessa

start here

Remember: while in public all dogs must wear a collar and tag and should be kept on a lead.

Remember: always take a poop-scoop bag with you and clean up after your dog.

"Yummy yummy! Three big juicy bones for me," says Tessa, but can you help her find her way through the maze to find the bones?

Who's walking who?
George is walking _____
Michelle is walking _____
Chris is walking _____

Drawing dogs and cats

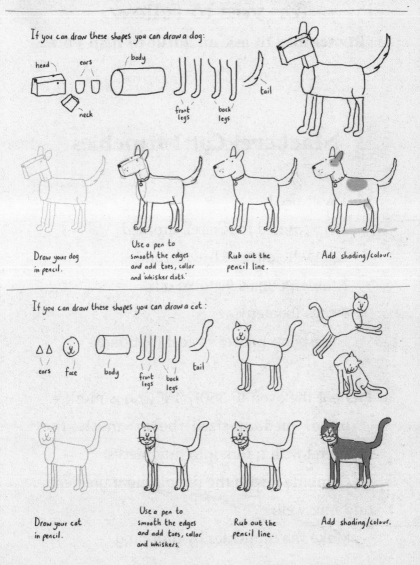

If you can draw these shapes you can draw a dog:

head
ears
body
neck
front legs
back legs
tail

Draw your dog in pencil.

Use a pen to smooth the edges and add toes, collar and 'whisker dots.'

Rub out the pencil line.

Add shading/colour.

If you can draw these shapes you can draw a cat:

ears
face
body
front legs
back legs
tail

Draw your cat in pencil.

Use a pen to smooth the edges and add toes, collar and whiskers.

Rub out the pencil line.

Add shading/colour.

Here is a delicious recipe for you to follow.

Remember to ask an adult to help you.

Mackerel Cat Munchies

You will need:

- 115g canned mackerel, drained
- 120g wholewheat breadcrumbs
- 2 tablespoons vegetable oil
- 2 eggs (beaten)
- 1 teaspoon brewer's yeast (optional)

Preheat the oven to 350F/ 180C/ gas mark 4.

In a medium-sized bowl, mash the mackerel with a fork into tiny pieces.

Combine it with the remaining ingredients and mix well.

Make the munchies by dropping

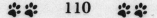

teaspoonful-sized dollops of the mixture onto a greased baking tray.

Bake for 8 minutes.

Once cooked, remove from the oven and cool to room temperature, then store in an airtight container in the fridge.

BATTERSEA DOGS & CATS HOME

There are lots of fun things on the
website, including an online quiz, e-cards,
colouring sheets and recipes for making
dog and cat treats.

www.battersea.org.uk